George The Wombat

A Potty Companion

This book belongs to:

_____

_____

_____

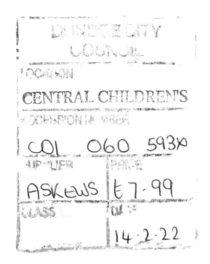
George the Wombat – A Potty Companion
Published in Great Britain in 2021 by Graffeg Limited.

First published by Mladá Fronta, Czech Republic 2016.

Written by Eva Papoušková © 2016.
Illustrated by Galina Miklínová © 2016.

Designed and produced by Graffeg Limited © 2021.

Translation into English by Alexandra Büchler.

Graffeg Limited, 24 Stradey Park Business Centre,
Mwrwg Road, Llangennech, Llanelli, Carmarthenshire,
SA14 8YP, Wales, UK. Tel: 01554 824000.
www.graffeg.com.

Eva Papoušková and Galina Miklínová are hereby
identified as the authors of this work in accordance with
section 77 of the Copyrights, Designs and Patents Act
1988.

A CIP Catalogue record for this book is available from
the British Library.

All rights reserved. No part of this publication may be
reproduced, stored in a retrieval system or transmitted,
in any form or by any means, electronic, mechanical,
photocopying, recording or otherwise, without the prior
permission of the publishers.

The publisher acknowledges the financial support of the
Books Council of Wales. www.gwales.com

ISBN 9781914079689

1 2 3 4 5 6 7 8 9

MIX
Paper from
responsible sources
FSC® C014138
FSC
www.fsc.org

Eva Papoušková & Galina Miklínová

GEORGE THE WOMBAT

A Potty Companion

GRAFFEG

What's a Wombat?

The Common wombat (*Vombatus ursinus*) is a hairy, slightly squat, chubby little animal with short legs. It is quite cute and very rare. Wombats live in Australia and are protected by law. Maybe this is because they are the only species on the planet that produce cube-shaped poos. We each have something that makes us unique.

One sunny morning George the Wombat wanted to
go and dig a burrow in the forest. But he also needed
to do something else.

'First you must do a number two!' said Mummy Wombat,
passing him the potty.

The little wombat sighed, but did as he was told
and sat down.

Sitting on his own he got really, REALLY bored.

Luckily his friend, Fred the kangaroo, happened to be passing.

'Hi George! Quick, come with me, let's go and fill our tummies with grass!'

'I can't,' replied George gloomily. 'I have to use the potty.'

'Go on then!' encouraged Fred.

'I'm trying, ' replied George, 'but nothing's happening.'

'Maybe you need to move about a bit' suggested Fred.
'Try running around the potty.'

So George got up and ran around the potty. Twice.

Then he sat back down and concentrated really hard.

But there was still no poo in sight.

Eventually, Fred got tired of waiting and hopped off to graze on his own...

... while George kept sitting on the potty.

After a while Annie the goose came by.

'George, do you want to come to the lagoon with me?
I have a nest there and I'm going to lay some eggs!'

George shook his head.

'I can't. I have to do a poo first, but it's not going well.'

'You need to drink a lot of water,' Annie told him, and she
took a bottle out from under her wing.

The little wombat drank and drank until the bottle was
empty.

Then he sat back down and concentrated really, REALLY
hard. But there was still no poo.

Annie also got tired of waiting and went off to lay her
eggs on her own...

... while George kept sitting on the potty.

Then Lizzie the mouse came by.

'What are you doing sitting there like that, George?'
she asked.

'I have to do a poo,' replied the little wombat,
'But it really isn't going well.'

'Try to push,' advised Lizzie. 'But please, wait until
I'm gone so I don't have to smell it.'

Lizzie quickly scampered off and George started to push.

He pushed, and pushed… until he pushed so hard his eyes almost popped out!

'George, why are you sitting here with your eyes popping out?' asked Daddy Wombat as he walked by on his way to go digging.

'I'm trying to do a poo, but it's not going well,' panted George.

They both looked into the potty. And, indeed, there was nothing there.

Daddy Wombat shook his head.

'If you sit here much longer the Tasmanian Devil will come and get you!' he warned.

That gave George a proper fright. Tasmanian devils are scary creatures. They come at you and growl and bite.

All of a sudden, something inside him started to grumble...

...and rumble...

... then something went 'plop' in the potty.

Mummy Wombat came running, George the Wombat stood up...
and the whole wombat family peered down.

'There you go!' said Mummy Wombat cheerfully.

'You've made a beautiful cube!'

George smiled. Now he could go and dig with his dad.